THE PANINIS

OF

POMPEII

PRAISE FOR **MR GUM**

PRAISE FOR **NATBOFF!**

THE PANINIS

OF
POMPEII

ANDY STANTON

Illustrated by Sholto Walker

EGMONT

EGMONT

We bring stories to life

First published in Great Britain MMXIX
by Egmont UK Limited
The Yellow Building, 1 Nicholas Road, London W11 4AN

Text copyright © MMXIX Andy Stanton
Illustrations copyright © MMXIX Sholto Walker

The moral rights of the author and illustrator have been asserted

978 1 4052 9385 3
70310/001

A CIP catalogue record for this title is available
from the British Library

Printed and bound in Great Britain by the CPI Group

Stay safe online. Any website addresses listed in this book are correct at
the time of going to print. However, Egmont is not responsible for content
hosted by third parties. Please be aware that online content can be subject to
change and websites can contain content that is unsuitable for children.
We advise that all children are supervised when using the internet.

Egmont takes its responsibility to the planet and its inhabitants very seriously.
We aim to use papers from well-managed forests run by responsible suppliers.

*For Polly, Luke and Sonny; and for Clemmy,
the greediest cat in Londinium – AS*

For Louis. Ut tibi auxillo esse ridiculam – SW

CONTENTS

CAECILIUS·AND
HIS·FAMILY

Now, back in Roman Times there lived a fat merchant by the name of Caecilius Maximus Panini. Caecilius was so fat that he looked a bit like a large football with a face on top, and this is what the name 'Caecilius' means: large football with a face on top. Caecilius had a lovely wife called

Vesuvius, which means 'Woman married to a guy who looks like a large football with a face on top'. And he had a little son called Filius, which means 'Filius'. Filius was ten years old, or as the Romans said, he was X years old. The Romans were always using letters instead of numbers and do you know why? It was because they were very stupid people indeed.

Now, not only was Caecilius a fat merchant – he was a fart merchant too. You see, like many businessmen of that time, Caecilius was in the fart trade. He would buy farts down the market on a Friderificus morning for two buzzle-swuzzles each (buzzle-swuzzles were the names of the coins in those days), and then on Saturanium – yes, the very next day! – he'd return to the market and sell them back to the same people he'd just bought them off – but this time for five buzzle-swuzzles each.

In this way, Caecilius had grown immensely rich. And he now had over thirty thousand buzzle-swuzzles in the bank. Thirty thousand buzzle-swuzzles! Can you imagine it? That's nearly five hundred cromps! This meant that Caecilius was one of the richest men alive. And you might be thinking to yourself that this is why he was so fat, you know, because he was always eating fancy foods and having toffees between mealtimes. But shame on you if you thought that. Caecilius was actually a fairly sensible eater, he just had a glandular problem.

Caecilius and his family lived in the town of Pompeii. Can you see how there's two 'i's at the end of the end of 'Pompeii' when surely one would be enough? The Ancient Romans were so rich and wasteful that they didn't even care how many letters they used! Nowadays we're far more careful with the way we use our letterssssssssssssssssssssssssssss

-sssssssssssssssssssssssssssssssssssssssssssssssssssssssssssssss

-sssssssssssssssssssssssssssssssssssssssssssssssssssssssssssssssss

-s.

LIFE·IN POMPEII

Pompeii was a very nice town, there were some impressive buildings and public spaces and a man who could make amazing animal noises simply by getting an animal and pulling its tail really hard – but there was one problem with living there. You see, there was a big volcano right next door to it.

'I don't like the look of that volcano,' said Caecilius one morning, looking out the window by standing near the window and pointing his face in the right direction and looking out the window. 'It could go off at any moment.'

'Mother,' said Filius, who was a bright and curious child, 'what is the name of that volcano?'

'No one knows,' replied Vesuvius, 'but your father is quite correct about it being a terrible menace. Only the other day I saw some pizzas come

VI

flying out of it. And quite a few Mirror-Men into the bargain.'

'Not those blasted Mirror-Men again, there seem to be more of them every year,' said Caecilius. 'Filius, my boy, can you go and fetch my sandals, I forgot to bring them inside and I'm afraid they're being eaten, or worn, by dogs.'

So Filius went to collect his father's sandals and while he did so, he thought about the Mirror-Men and about all the other inventions that the Romans had come up with. You see, the Romans were very clever people indeed and they had invented lots of things that we still use today, including: central heating; baths; frogs; roads; pencils with rubbers on the end; Mirror-Men; Mirror-Men with central heating; Mirror-

Men with rubbers on the end; frogs with central heating; baths with Mirror-Men sitting in them; roads covered with pencils and frogs; aqueducts; aqueducts filled with Mirror-Men pencils with rubbers on the end; spears; spears with rubbers on the end; Mirror-Men eating spears and frogs; volcanoes; pizzas; pizzas erupting out of volcanoes; pizzas erupting out of frogs; frogs erupting out of pizzas; roads with central heating; Mirror-Men sitting on a giant pizza erupting out of a volcano,

near a frog; baths but when you turn on the tap, pencils come out instead of water; togas (which were a kind of robe that everyone wore) and toga-rones (which were a kind of robe made of chocolate and instead  of taking it off when you went to bed you just ate it and a new one grew back the next day, I think).

Some of the inventions were useful (e.g. pencils with rubbers on the end) and some were brilliant (e.g. pizzas and frogs) and some were terrible (e.g. volcanoes) and some were a mixture of brilliant and terrible (e.g. pizzas erupting out of volcanoes, because someone could get hurt. Or even if they didn't, even if the pizza didn't land on you and burn your face off, even if it landed on the ground, would

you want to eat a pizza that had landed on the ground? At the very least it would be quite dusty) and some were just no one really understood them at all (e.g. Mirror-Men).

Most of the time it was brilliant being a Roman because the Holy Roman Empire ruled the world and if you were a Roman you were allowed to do an army and go to any country you liked and kick people. But some of the inventions were more trouble than they were worth. They had gotten out of hand.

The Mirror-Men in particular were very bothersome. One night Caecilius was having a bath and he found about thirty of the things sitting in there holding pencils with rubbers on the end. The next night there were more like forty Mirror-Men in there with him and the night after that there were nearly seventy thousand. There were so many Mirror-Men that Caecilius could hardly fit in the tub to have a bath and he just had to lick himself clean like a cat, or an ice cream that has somehow learned to eat its own body to survive. And to make matters worse, while he was licking himself clean, a nearby volcano (not the main one, but another one) exploded in a shower of pizzas, frogs, central heating, roads, aqueducts and yet more Mirror-Men.

'Drat and figs!' yelled Caecilius, kicking the bathtub out of the window and into the garden, where it landed on Caecilius's head, even though he was actually the one standing in the bathroom who had kicked the bathtub out of the window in the first place so I don't know how that happened, probably just physics wasn't very proper in those times.

'Ow!' cried Caecilius, rubbing his head with a pencil with a rubber on the end. You'd think the rubber would be good for rubbing his head, but actually it started erasing it.

'This day is going from bad to worse!' yelled Caecilius. 'Everything exploding all the time! Mirror-Men everywhere! And now I've erased most of my own head!'

So that's what life in Roman Times was like. Good, but they had their problems.

CAECILIUS
AND·BARKUS
WOOFERINICUM

Now, Caecilius's son Filius had a dog whom he'd found in a bath one day, and this scraggy devil went by the name of Barkus Wooferinicum. He had a horrid pointed snout and you could see his ribs poking through. Caecilius didn't trust Barkus

Wooferinicum but Filius loved him so the dog stayed. Mostly he slept out on the streets.

One morning, Caecilius got up at dawn to try to get the best bargains on the farts at the market, and this is where the phrase 'the early Caecilius gets the fart' comes from. He got out of bed, fondly stroked Vesuvius's hair and put on his toga, sandals and Julius Caesar pendant.

Then he jumped out of the window on to the street below and broke both his legs.

'Ouch,' said Caecilius, 'I wish I hadn't done that.'

Caecilius took out his magic charm, which had been given to him by a dirty rabbit, and spoke the words:

'*Go back in time, go back in time, go back in time, that's what I want to do.*'

Immediately the magic charm lit up and Caecilius was transported back to his warm bed, ready to have another go at going out. His legs were absolutely fine.

So, just as before, he got out of bed, fondly stroked Vesuvius's hair and put on his toga, sandals and Julius Caesar pendant. Then he jumped out of the window on to the street below and broke both his legs.

'Ouch,' said Caecilius. 'I really thought I wouldn't break my legs that time.'

Once more he took out his magic charm and spoke the words:

'Go back in time, go back in time, go back in time, that's what I want to do.'

Once more the magic charm lit up and Caecilius found himself back in his warm bed and ready to face the day.

So, for a third time, he got out of bed, fondly stroked Vesuvius's hair and put on his toga, sandals and Julius Caesar pendant. This time Caecilius decided to walk down the stairs and thus he proceeded outside at last. The sun was coming up over Pompeii. In the distance a small volcano erupted and six hundred Mirror-Men came out, about average for that time of morning.

Caecilius turned left at the end of the road, then left again, then left once more and then finally left again. This meant he had walked around the block and arrived back at his own front door. It wasn't very useful for getting to the market but, quite by accident, Caecilius had done an astounding thing — he had invented the square! So whenever you see a square, such as a town square or a sandwich or something else which is square, just think — if it hadn't been for Caecilius, life would have been very different. And this is why Caecilius's name means 'The Man Who Invented the Square'. ('Cae' means 'The Man' and 'lius' means 'Who Invented the

Square' and the 'ci' bit in the middle is just there for decoration and glue.) Would you like to see a square right now? Here's one.

Would you like to see another twenty of them?

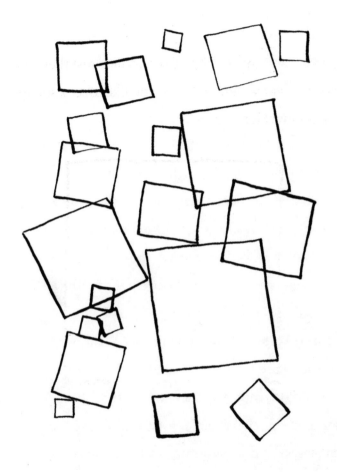

Here they are, they're good, aren't they? The man who is drawing them is called Sholto Walker. I can make him draw squares any time I feel like it.

On walked Caecilius, laughing as he did so, for he had just thought of a brilliant joke to play on Vesuvius.

I shall put a gherkin in Vesuvius's shoe when she isn't looking, thought Caecilius. *And then, when she puts her foot in her shoe, she will say, 'Oh, what's this? There is something in my shoe.' And then she'll look inside and get the surprise of her life when she sees nothing other than – a GHERKIN!*

But as Caecilius was chuckling to himself, up rushed Barkus Wooferinicum, who had been lying in wait since the very first line of the story, waiting for just this moment, and now he flew through the air, not real flying but the type of flying that just means he did a big jump, and he sank his strong teeth into Caecilius's hairy arm.

'That looks painful,' said Onlyappearsinone-otherchapterus the candle-maker, who happened to be passing by at that moment. 'Oh well, see you later.'

'Ouch! Miserable cur!' shouted Caecilius and he pulled out a fig and with it he beat Barkus Wooferinicum to death.

'Get up, you silly dog,' commanded Caecilius, but then he realised that Barkus Wooferinicum was actually dead.

'Oh, no,' sobbed the fart merchant, 'I never meant to kill the hound, this was nothing more than an over-enthusiastic figging.'

Suddenly Caecilius remembered his magic charm! He pulled it out and said the words:

'*Go back in time, go back in time, go back in time, that's what I want to do.*'

But the magic charm didn't light up. It had only had two goes in it and Caecilius had wasted them both on saving his own legs.

'Drat,' said Caecilius. 'I'd better not let Filius find out about this, or he'll be upset.'

So Caecilius quickly stuffed the dead dog under his toga and ran back to the villa as fast as he could, which wasn't very fast because he had a dead dog under his toga. In fact, I forgot to tell you this but actually he had forty-eight dead dogs under his toga, because before Barkus Wooferinicum had attacked him, forty-seven other dogs had attacked him too – one at a time, each after the other – and each time, Caecilius had beaten them to death with a fig.

As Caecilius was waddling unsteadily through the front door, Filius came out, ready to go off to school.

'*Salve*, Father,' said Filius. 'I wonder why you have got forty-eight tails sticking out from under your toga.'

'They are not tails,' said Caecilius, thinking fast,
'but hairy loaves of bread which I am keeping warm
for our ugly friends, Atrium and Hortus.'

'Oh, OK,' said Filius. 'By the way, Father, have you seen Barkus Wooferinicum, by the way, by the way, Father? By the way?'

'"Barkus Wooferinicum"?' said Caecilius, thinking quickly once more. 'What is that? Is it the title of a new play at the theatre?'

'No, Father,' said Filius. 'It is my dog, do you remember?'

'Hmm,' frowned Caecilius. 'Well, *I've* never heard of him, are you sure you had a dog?'

'Yes,' said Filius, 'I'm certain. I've had him for about a year, remember?'

'Are you absolutely sure though?' said Caecilius. 'Memory can play strange tricks of the mind on your mind. Perhaps you only thought you had a dog, when in actual fact you really had nothing more than an ant.'

'No, he was definitely a dog,' sighed Filius. 'Oh,

well, I'd better go off to school.'

'Drat and figs,' said Caecilius as he waddled through the villa into the back garden. 'Filius is a bright boy. I tried to fool him into thinking he'd never had a dog but he wasn't having any of it.'

The next four hours were very boring for Caecilius because he spent them digging an enormous hole in the lawn, using only his big toes. Then he threw all the dead dogs in and covered them over with earth, using only his big toes. But when it was done, he had a horrible realisation, using only his big toes.

Filius will come back from school at lunchtime, Caecilius's big toes thought to themselves, *and he will expect to play with Barkus Wooferinicum. And when the dog is not to be found, he will grow suspicious. And when he grows suspicious, he will grow more suspicious. And when he has grown more suspicious, he will grow even more suspicious and start asking questions. And when he has asked all the questions, we don't know what he will do next, we are only big toes and not that clever.*

But still, Caecilius and his big toes were on the right track – if Barkus Wooferinicum were not around at lunchtime, Filius would soon discover the awful truth that his animal friend was no longer of this earth, but was instead under this earth.

Now, at that moment, a dog which looked *exactly like* Barkus Wooferinicum happened to walk through the garden and this gave Caecilius a crafty idea. In a flash he pounced on the animal and shaved off all its fur, using a fig. Then he stuck the fur all over his own body and waited for Filius to come home for lunch.

Soon Filius came home for lunch.

Exactly what I was waiting for, thought Caecilius.

'*Salve*, Filius,' he heard Vesuvius say from the kitchen, where she was busy sticking together thousands and thousands of pencils with a rubber on the end so that she could reach up into the sky and draw a face on the moon. (It took Vesuvius another week of sticking pencils together but eventually she managed it, and she drew a very fine face on the moon indeed. And even today, if you look up at the moon you will be able to see the face that Vesuvius drew all those years ago! We know him as 'The Man in the Moon' but she called him 'Bobbling Ed'.)

27

'How was your morning at school?'

'It was excellent,' said Filius. 'We learnt about a brand-new shape that's just been invented. It is called a "square". Now, where is my faithful dog, I wish to play with him – ah, there you are,' he beamed, as Caecilius came running in to the kitchen on all fours, barking merrily away.

Well, Filius and 'Barkus Wooferinicum' played together for the whole lunch hour that day.

And the next day, and the next day too. This went on for over three weeks, and then Caecilius began to get bored.

'Vesuvius,' he said to his wife one evening as they were preparing for bed, 'I have done something dreadful.'

And he told her the whole sorry story of how he had accidentally killed Barkus Wooferinicum and forty-seven other dogs. And how, rather than admit this to Filius, he had instead been dressing up as a dog for the past three weeks.

'I am a turtle fighter,' sighed Caecilius. 'I mean, I am a terrible father.' He scooped up a grade 'B' fart and looked at it sadly. 'No, no, I don't even deserve this,' he sighed, and threw the fart down the toilet, which for farts is a sort of nightclub where they can dance with all their friends.

'Perhaps you are not as terrible as you think, my dear husband,' smiled Vesuvius, and she flung open the window with her mind to reveal an unexpected sight. It was Filius, and he was playing with forty-eight dogs in the garden. And the biggest and shiniest of all the dogs was –

'Barkus Wooferinicum!' laughed Caecilius. 'He's not dead at all! And neither are the other dogs I thought I'd killed!'

'Actually the other forty-seven dogs *are* dead,' said Vesuvius sadly. 'The ones Filius is playing with are a different forty-seven dogs. But you are quite right – Barkus Wooferinicum himself is absolutely fine.'

'See, Father, you only stunned him with that fig!' cried Filius from the garden.

'So you knew the whole story all along,' laughed Caecilius, fondly stroking his son's hair even though he wasn't standing anywhere near Filius and couldn't possibly have reached him. 'And yet you made me dress up as a dog for three whole weeks!'

31

'Yes, Father,' replied Filius seriously. 'For the moral of Ancient Pompeii is this: *"Be thou honest in thy dealings".*'

'It is true,' said Caecilius thoughtfully. 'I was not honest with you, Filius, and for that I apologise. I am sorry I killed your dog.'

'But you didn't kill him, remember?' said Filius.

'Oh, yes,' said Caecilius. 'Well, then, I am sorry I didn't kill your dog.'

'Hold on,' said Filius, 'you're sorry you *didn't* kill him?'

'No, that came out wrong,' said Caecilius, 'but the important thing is, I'm tired, I'm going to bed. Goodnighticus, everyoneicus.'

So Caecilius and Vesuvius went to bed and slept, and dreamt their happy dreams. Caecilius dreamt he was a chef.

The next morning Vesuvius woke up and when

she put on her shoe, she said, 'Oh, what's this? There is something in my shoe.' And when she looked inside she got the surprise of her life because she found nothing other than –

'A GHERKIN!' cried Vesuvius, aghast. 'How in the name of Jupiter did that get there?'

But only one man in the whole of Pompeii knew the answer, and that man was already well on his way to market to get the early fart, chuckling as he went.

THE·END

FILIUS
AND·SLAVIUS

Now, Filius had everything he could possibly want in life – a pencil with a rubber on the end, some Mirror-Men and something else. All sorts of things. He even had a dice and when you threw it, it controlled the weather. I was sunny, II was cloudy, III was storms, IV was rainbows you could eat, V was overcast and VI was all the weather at once. But still Filius was bored, because children with everything often have nothing, in a way.

'I am bored, Barkus Wooferinicum,' said Filius. 'Why don't you do that trick you like doing, to cheer me up?'

So Barkus Wooferinicum did his trick but it didn't really cheer Filius up because the trick was just to carry on behaving normally.

'Drat and figs,' said Filius, who had learned this naughty expression from his father. 'I think I am going to go crazy with boredom, you know.'

But just then he heard someone else saying 'Drat and figs!' in the next room. His curiosity roused, Filius crept along the corridor and peered in to the front room, where Slavius the household slave was looking gloomy, as if someone had rolled a V on his face.

'Drat and figs,' sighed Slavius. 'I am so bored

being a slave. I wish I could be anyone else – yes, even that spoilt brat, Filius – just for one day. I bet if I were Filius, everything would be all right.'

Now, this gave Filius an extremely crafty idea. He ran into the room and smashed Slavius over the head with an enormous Roman vase.

'That's for calling me a spoilt brat,' said Filius. And then he had another crafty idea.

'Let us change places, you and I,' said Filius. 'For just one day, you shall be me and I shall be you.'

'I see,' said Slavius. 'Your plan is a delight, for we look quite similar, you and I. So now let us change our togas. And a-ho, a-ha! We each are the other one now! I am Filius!' said Slavius, clapping his hands in glee.

'And a-ho, a-ha! I am Slavius!' announced Filius. Then Slavius (dressed as Filius) smashed a massive vase over Filius's head.

'What was that for?' said Filius (dressed as Slavius).

'That's for calling me a spoilt brat,' laughed Slavius. 'For I am now you and you me, remember?'

Just then Caecilius's car pulled into the driveway (the Romans did not have cars, of course, 'car' was just short for 'carrot'). Caecilius and Vesuvius had been out all afternoon in their carrot, with their ugly friends, Atrium and Hortus.

'I don't even know why we are friends with those dreadful people,' grumbled Vesuvius as she and her husband slipped through the front door. 'All Hortus ever does is go on and on about her scented herb gardens, even though I've never heard of her scented herb gardens – if she even has any – and in actual fact she never goes on about them at all. But I bet she will, in a later story.'

'There, there,' said Caecilius, fondly stroking his wife's hair. Then he glanced at the sundial on his wrist.

'By the Gods of Honey and Fig Mountain!' he cried. 'We shall be late for the theatre. Filius, Filius, my lad, come along, look lively!'

'Quick,' said the real Filius in the front room. 'Slavius, you must go with them and pretend to be me.'

'And you must go to the Tavern of the Slaves,'

grinned Slavius, 'and pretend to be me, for I promised my friend Agricola that I would be there tonight to make merry with him.'

'Then the game is on,' said the real Filius, quickly smashing a vase over the real Slavius's head.

'What was that for?' asked Slavius.

'I'm not really sure,' admitted Filius, who had lost track of who should be smashing who over the head with enormous Roman vases. 'Now, go! And may the luck of the Gods go with you!'

'You too,' laughed the real Slavius, and running into the hallway he said, '*Salve*, Mother and Father. It is me, your little son, Filius, ready to accompany you to the theatre!'

'Then let us proceed there at once,' said Caecilius, and catching hold of a passing dove he announced, 'We shall travel by dove!'

But the dove was unable to bear the weight of

three people and so they walked to the theatre instead.

As soon as they were gone, Filius (disguised as Slavius) leapt out of his hiding-place and ran outdoors.

'Ha!' he shouted at the evening sky. 'What fun it is to be a slave! I have never felt so free!'

And off he headed for the Tavern of the Slaves to experience life in another world.

Walking through the theatre doors, Slavius (disguised as Filius) could barely believe his eyes. 'It is so big and grand,' he marvelled. 'What are we here to see?'

'We are going to watch a startling new play called *The Boy Who Lied to Some People Who Trusted*

Him,' said Caecilius.

'That sounds exciting,' said Slavius. 'Shall we go and sit down?'

'Yes,' replied Caecilius, 'but first – don't you want some of your favourite theatre snacks?'

'Yes, please, Father,' replied Slavius, 'what are they again, I've forgotten.'

'Why, it's strawberries, that's what you love,' laughed Vesuvius. 'Here, let me buy you the biggest basket that money will buy.'

And the three of them entered the theatre with Slavius silently cheering to himself, as if someone had rolled a I inside his soul.

'Strawberries and entertainment,' he thought. 'Certainly is it a fact that indeed this is surely the life for me, most excellently and decidedly so in truth!'

Meanwhile, Filius (disguised as Slavius) had reached the Tavern of the Slaves, which was a lowly building, which meant it stank. The floor was covered with sawdust and broken pencils with rubbers on the end lying about, and none of the Mirror-Men had been tidied for months, but just lay heaped in a corner gathering dust and laying eggs.

All the same, Filius was enchanted.

'Back at the villa everything is so clean and neat and dull,' he marvelled. 'Truly, this where the life is – with these lowly, reeking people and their crude games and challenges.'

'Aha!' bellowed a voice into Filius's ear just then. 'Slavius! I knew you would show up. Good to see you, mate.'

Filius turned and saw a fellow not much older than himself. He was startled to see it was Agricola, the slave belonging to his parents' ugly friends, Atrium and Hortus.

'Agricola, do not address me in so familiar a manner,' said Filius angrily. 'Go and fetch me some farts – and look quick about it or next time it shall not be merely the sharpness of my tongue you feel, but the keen cut of my whip, you insolent goat.'

'Why,' marvelled Agricola, 'you talk to me as if you were not a slave yourself, but instead a young master, such as that spoilt brat Filiu– ouch, why did you just smash an enormous Roman vase over my head?'

'Never mind,' said Filius. 'Now, look, Agricola. I'm sorry I spoke to you like a young master. It was just a sort of a joke. I am actually a slave like you. Now, let us sit and scoop up a fart or two and talk about what slaves like to talk of.'

Filius sat himself down on one of the mean chairs

of that place and regarded the soiled and crusty table with interest. Agricola went to the bar and returned holding a couple of farts, one of which he offered to Filius. But Filius was struck with a dumb sort of horror such as he had rarely known.

Why, he thought, *I have never seen such a low-*

grade fart in all my life. It is full of gristle and bone, and see! It hardly swirls but lies in Agricola's hand like a tired mouse! I can barely bring myself to scoop it up.

'Aaaah,' said Agricola. 'Look at that, would you? A grade 'E', what a treat.'

'But it is hardly even fit for a dog such as Barkus Wooferinicum,' shouted Filius, 'do not touch it a moment longer!' and, rising, he swatted at the fart and sent it flying from Agricola's hand through the window, where it immediately scurried away into the shadows.

'I do not know what has got into you tonight, Slavius!' exclaimed Agricola, also rising. 'You, who are usually so fond of the Tavern of the Slaves, have treated everything as if it were beneath you. Shame, shame, shame, shame, shame, shame, shame on you! Yes, you heard me, Slavius, I have brought the Seven Shames of the Slaves upon you. One for

Pride, two for Loathsome Thoughts, Three for Vile Countenance, Four for Moral Indecision, Five for Being Weak of Flesh, Six for Idle Hands and Seven for Foolish Doltery! Yes, Slavius – I pronounce upon you the Seven Shames of the Slaves, and each more shameful than the last.'

'Blast him to the Gods,' cried the other slaves, and soon a full-fledged brawl was in progress, with Filius and Agricola at the centre of the ruckus.

※ ⁂ ※

'I do not think I like this play,' said the real Slavius, back at the theatre.

'Hush, it is an excellent entertainment,' said Caecilius, 'and look you well to the moral of the story, which is coming up now.'

On stage, the actor was weeping and wailing.

XLVI

'Oh, woe, woe,' said he, 'I am undone. For I once was a good boy – a simple slave to a family who cared for me and gave me shelter and some ham. But I have lied to them. I have disguised myself as their son and now the Gods will punish me.'

'That is correct,' said a huge face made of wood. It was only a play, but Slavius was completely terrified for he had never been to the theatre before and his simple slave's mind could hardly tell the difference between truth and fiction.

'I am the mighty god, JUPITER,' thundered the face on the stage. 'Now, you naughty boy who lied to the very people who trusted him – I will thwart you. For you have eaten strawberries which you did pluck from my enchanted forest, and which you did think were so sweet. But no, it was all a trap, I have made them as bitter and poisonous as your lies themselves, and now you shall perish from eating them.'

'It is all I deserve,' wept the actor on the stage, and he fell to his knees and rolled on to his side.

'And now, because of my lies – I die.'

'No, no,' shouted Slavius from his seat. 'I cannot stand it any longer. It is all I deserve! It is all I deserve!

Yes, these strawberries – I can feel them, burning me up inside, just like the deceitful boy in the play. Oh, I can feel them inside me, what agony! I must die, I must surely die!'

And, scattering strawberries everywhere, he leapt from his seat and ran from the theatre into the dark night beyond.

Meanwhile, the real Filius was racing away from the Tavern of the Slaves with Agricola and the rest of his fellows in hot pursuit, throwing tables, chairs, farts, Mirror-Men, tankards, vases and a tree at him.

'Think you're better than us, Slavius?' they yelled. 'We'll show you!'

The terrified lad rounded the corner – only to

collide with the real Slavius as he fled the theatre in tears.

'You!' said Filius.

'You!' said Slavius.

'Quick, we must change back,' breathed Filius. 'I cannot cope with your life of quick tempers and low-grade farts.'

'And I for my part cannot stand the incredible

morals and meaningful strawberries of high society,' declared Slavius.

In a flash, they exchanged togas, and now they stood in the middle of the street as the slaves came running up on one side, and Caecilius and Vesuvius approached from the other.

'Calm down, everyone,' said Filius. 'There is no need to fight nor to be angry. For you see before you two simple fools – one high born, the other a common slave – who each thought he would be better off in the other's sandals.'

'But we were wrong,' said Slavius. 'For the moral of Ancient Pompeii is this: *"No person should be unhappy with his lot".'*

'Well, I don't really understand,' said Caecilius, stroking Filius's and Slavius's hair fondly, 'but I am glad to have my son back and the two of you shall go unpunished on this occasion.'

'And we are glad to have our friend Slavius back,' said the slaves.

'Hooray!' cried Filius and he took out his dice and rolled a III.

'Oh, it's storms,' he said as it began to thunder and rain.

'It does not matter,' said Caecilius, stroking the thunder's hair fondly as they walked back to the villa, Filius and Slavius arm-in-arm like brothers. 'It is only weather, it does not mean that the story turned out unhappily.'

And they all laughed, for Caecilius was right, and they went back to the villa and never again did Filius and Slavius swap places. But from that day forth, each understood the other's life a little better. Filius stopped smashing enormous vases over Slavius's head *quite* so often, and for his part, Slavius more or less stopped gossiping about

Filius and referring to him as 'a horrid little poo face' behind his back.

T H E · E N D

THE · MA-WOL-N-F

Now, this story is a spooky affair, and it all has to do with a dinner party that Caecilius and his lovely wife Vesuvius were throwing for some friends of the family, an ugly couple called Atrium and Hortus.

The dinner had been very successful. Everyone

had enjoyed a lovely meal of olives and some cheese made from the hind leg of a goat, and now it was time to sit back and undo your toga and let your belly flop where it would. Slavius collected up the empty dishes and took them into the kitchen to be licked to a sparkling shine by Barkus Wooferinicum, for the Romans valued health and hygiene above all other things. Everyone was in a pleasant mood.

'After-dinner fart?' said Caecilius, offering around a tray of Grade 'A' quality farts he'd been saving for just such an occasion.

'Don't mind if I do,' said Atrium, scooping one up.

'Me neither,' said Hortus.

'Can I have a fart too, Mother?' asked little Filius.

'Now, now, Filius,' said Vesuvius. 'You're only X.'

'Oh, go on, give the boy a fart,' said Caecilius,

stroking his son's hair fondly. 'It's not often he gets to stay up late with the adults, what harm's a fart going to do him?'

'Oh, Caecilius, you are a big softie,' laughed Vesuvius. 'OK, Filius, you can have I fart, but only I.'

'Ah, there's nothing like a good Pompeiian fart,' pronounced Atrium as he popped a particularly juicy specimen into his mouth. 'A finer blow-off you could not find in Rome itself!'

'That reminds me,' said Vesuvius. 'How *was* your recent trip to Rome?'

'It was simply perfect,' replied Atrium. 'We had a marvellous time.'

'Yes, it is an extraordinary city,' volunteered Hortus. 'Did you know, they built it in a day?'

'I'd love to see Rome,' said Vesuvius, turning to her husband. 'We must visit sometime, mustn't we, dear?'

'We must indeed,' agreed Caecilius, stroking Vesuvius's hair fondly.

Wow, thought Filius in fascination. *Grown-ups' conversations are so boring.*

'Still, it's good to be back home,' said Atrium.
'And of course, Hortus missed her gardening while
we were away, didn't you, my love?'

But at this Hortus let out a dirty gasp.

'Oh!' she cried. 'That reminds me, I saw something awfully . . . strange the other night. But – no, no, it is too impossible, I must have imagined it.'

'What was it?' said Caecilius, stroking Hortus's hair fondly. 'Do tell us, for after dinner is just the time for stories, no matter how impossible or dull.'

'Well,' began Hortus. 'It did happen the other night that I was walking through my scented herb gardens – '

'I didn't know you had scented herb gardens,' said Vesuvius, 'although I suspected as much a few pages ago.'

'I am surprised, Vesuvius,' replied Hortus quite haughtily, 'for my scented herb gardens are quite famous throughout Pompeii.'

'They can't be *that* famous,' said Vesuvius. 'I've known you for ages and I've never heard of them.'

'Well, I am a little put out by that, to be honest,'

said Hortus. 'As I say, my scented herb gardens are really quite well known around here.'

'Yes,' Atrium chipped in, 'Hortus is very proud of her scented herb gardens.'

'I haven't heard of them either,' put in Filius at this point.

'Shh, my boy,' said Vesuvius in embarrassment. 'It's already bad enough that I haven't heard of Hortus's so-called "scented herb gardens" without you getting involved.'

'Hey,' said Hortus, 'what do you mean by that? What do you mean my "so-called" scented herb gardens?'

'I didn't mean anything by it,' said Vesuvius. 'I just think it's a bit suspicious that I haven't heard of these *incredibly famous* scented herb gardens.'

'Are you calling my wife a liar?' shouted Atrium. 'Are you? Because if you are, then why don't you just come out and say it? Why don't you just come out and say it, Vesuvius, you nasty piece of work? Instead of sitting there with that stupid smug grin on your face having a go at Hortus like that!'

'I wasn't "having a go" at anyone!' shouted Vesuvius. 'I just hadn't heard about these STUPID scented herb groves –'

'GARDENS,' shouted Hortus. 'Scented. Herb. GARDENS.'

'WHATEVER,' yelled Vesuvius. 'WHAT. EVER.'

'Calm down, calm down,' said Caecilius now, stroking everyone's hair fondly. 'I'm sure that no one meant anyone any harm. Come, Slavius!' he cried, clicking his belly twice in rapid succession. 'Bring us more farts – no, none for you, Filius, you hopeful lad! – bring us more farts and we will forget our differences.'

After all the adults had each scooped up another fart or two, Hortus began to tell her tale again.

'As *some* of you may know,' she began, 'I have some scented herb gardens, which are actually *quite well regarded* in these parts. But never mind, I'm sure you can't be expected to pay heed to *everything* that goes on around here, Vesuvius. Anyway, it was exactly a month ago, I remember that, because it was the night of the full moon. So there I was, walking through my –'

'*Scented herb gardens*,' muttered Vesuvius.

'Now, now, 'Suvie,' said Caecilius before Vesuvius could erupt once more. 'No need to be sarcastic. Do go on, Hortus.'

'Very well,' said Hortus. 'So there I was, wandering through my scented herb gardens, enjoying the scents. The wonderful perfume of the basil, the bright fresh aroma of the mint, the spicy oregano, the jade, the rosemary – all those lovely scents in the scented herb gardens.'

'Get on with it already,' said Vesuvius, rolling her eyes.

'Now,' continued Hortus, 'I had just come to my favourite part of the gardens – the coriander. And it was while I was bending down to sniff at that lovely herb that I heard it. A rustling in the undergrowth. And then I saw it. A huge, hairy PAW was peeking out from amongst the coriander bushes. And then the moon came out from behind a cloud – I hadn't realised it but I must have been in the scented herb gardens for much longer than I thought, for by now it was night time – and then I saw him. Or rather – *it.*'

'What? What was it?' gasped Filius, who was so terrified that he had accidentally done a Mirror-Man in his pants.

'It was like nothing I have ever seen before,' said

Hortus, a strange, far-away look on her ugly face. 'Or rather – it was like two things I have seen before, but never together. A man, it seemed to me! And yet – a wolf as well!'

'A ma-wol-n-f!' exclaimed Vesuvius.

'Yes,' agreed Hortus, gripping her friend's hand in hers, their argument now forgotten. 'It was a ma-wol-n-f! A terrible blending of two creatures, emerging slowly from the coriander. It smelt dreadful, Vesuvius! Dreadful! It smelt like a mixture of a man and a wolf! And a bit of coriander!'

'How tall was the beast?' demanded Caecilius in Russian – but no one understood.

'How tall was the beast?' he demanded again, not in Russian.

'It was about IX feet tall,' sobbed Hortus. 'And it had big jaws. And around its neck it wore a pendant.'

'A pendant with a portrait of Julius Caesar on, by any chance?' said Caecilius.

'Yes, h-how did you know?' cried Hortus.

But just then, night time fell and the house was plunged into darkness. And then, suddenly, the full moon came out from behind a cloud. And now the people at the table gasped, for Caecilius was gone! And in his place stood a cross between a wolf and a man – a ma-wol-n-f – standing there slobbering all over the table and scrabbling at the tiled floor with his dreadful claws.

'I can't believe it,' said Vesuvius. 'The beast is Caecilius.'

'Are you going to eat us?' shouted Atrium in outrage.

But the ma-wol-n-f only shook its head and cried hairy tears on to the table.

'It just wants to be loved,' said Vesuvius.

So they all stood there, fondly stroking the creature's shaggy brown hair. And later on, it turned back into Caecilius and they all had a great big laugh about it, and Filius managed to sneak down another fart when no one was looking and it made him drunk and he fell out the window; but luckily he landed on a family of Mirror-Men, which cushioned his fall – so everything worked out fine.

THE·END

AT·THE·BATHS

Now, Caecilius was a person who lived way back in Ancient Roman Times, I probably haven't mentioned that before but it's true. In fact, all of these stories are set in Ancient Roman Times, in a town called Pompeii. And they are illustrated for your pleasure by a man named Sholto Walker. Hey, Sholto, draw another square for me.

I can totally make Sholto draw squares any time I like.

Now, did you know that baths were very important to the Ancient Romans? Well, they were. Not just little baths like you or I have – but extraordinary public baths where all the men and women of the town would go. There they would bathe together in the health-giving waters, the men in one section of the building and the women in quite another. And more than this, the baths were a crucial part of Roman social life, a place where tall tales were told and scandalous gossip was gossiped and all sorts of enjoyable pastimes were indulged in: throwing spoons as high into the air as possible, for example, or trying to irritate the vulture.

So anyway, one day Caecilius was sitting around the Pompeii baths having a bit of a gossip with his ugly friend, Atrium. There were about four hundred other guys there as well, all completely naked. Filius was there, completely naked. Also, Barkus Wooferinicum was there, he was the only one wearing clothes because the rules of the baths clearly stated that all the men had to be naked but that all the dogs had to wear clothes. So Barkus Wooferinicum was wearing his favourite dress, actually it might not have been his favourite dress, actually he wasn't at the baths at all, I was mistaken, I thought he was but he wasn't. Actually he was there in a way. He was there in Filius's thoughts, because as everyone lay around the baths throwing spoons into the air and trying to irritate the vulture, Filius was thinking about Barkus Wooferinicum.

I like Barkus Wooferinicum, he is a nice dog, Filius was thinking.

'Quiet with your thoughts, my lad,' laughed Caecilius, turning down the volume on Filius's brain from VII to III. 'I am trying to have a gossip with Atrium and I can hardly hear what he has to say with you thinking of Barkus Wooferinicum all the time. Now, what was it you were saying, Atrium?'

'Well,' replied Atrium, and not only did he throw a spoon into the air, but when it came down it landed on the vulture's head, so that counted as two pastimes for the price of one. 'I shall tell you what I was saying, Caecilius, but I am afraid you must not call me "Atrium" any more. Because while you were speaking to Filius just now, I changed my name to "Frollicus".'

'Did you really?' said Caecilius in astonishment.

'Well then, Frollicus, what was it you were saying?'

'I am afraid I cannot answer that question,' replied Atrium/Frollicus. 'Because just before you asked me that question I changed my name again, this time to "Maltus Vinegarus".'

'What sport is this!' laughed Caecilius, fondly stroking Atrium's/Frollicus's/Maltus Vinegarus's curly hair. 'Well then, Maltus Vinegarus, I ask you now – what was it you were going to tell me?'

'Too slow,' laughed Caecilius's companion. 'For I have changed my name to Barkus Wooferinicum.'

'This is getting very tiresome,' Caecilius whispered to Filius. 'I think Atrium has gone mad, shall we go to the Honey Room?'

Now, the Honey Room was one of the finest rooms in the whole of the public baths. It was just a room but it was called the Honey Room, so it felt more special than the other rooms.

'OK,' said Filius, but then he happened to glance at his father's magnificent hairy chest and he let out a horrified poo.

'Father!' exclaimed Filius. 'What has become of the Julius Caesar pendant that you always wear around your neck? For it has disappeared as quickly as a bowl of olives and nuts set before a hungry senator!'

'Drat and figs!' shouted Caecilius so loudly that the walls of the public baths came tumbling down, killing thirty people.

'!sgif dna tarD' he quickly shouted, to make the walls come tumbling up again. Most of the people came back to life as well, except for a couple of old men whose bodies were so frail that they were unable to reassemble themselves in time.

'Drat and figs!' said Caecilius, speaking more quietly. 'There is only one explanation. A nimble-fingered thief walks amongst us, yes, here at the public baths where I did think all men were equal. If any man stole my pendant, or if any man does know who is the cur responsible, let him stand up now and admit the crime. For this is Ancient Rome, I mean it's Pompeii but you know, it's Ancient Roman Times. And this sort of thing is uncivilised.'

Then Caecilius went up to one man and said, 'We are not flies, buzzing around a pot of old goat meat, trying to get a sniff! We are civilised men and we shall not stand for this sort of errant behaviour.'

Then he went up to another man and said, 'We are not flies, buzzing around a pot of old goat meat, trying to get a sniff! We are civilised men and we shall not stand for this sort of errant behaviour.'

Then he went up to a third man and said, 'We are not flies, buzzing around a pot of old goat meat, trying to get a sniff! We are civilised men and we shall not stand for this sort of errant behaviour.'

Then he went up to a fourth man and said, 'We are not flies, buzzing around a pot of old goat meat, trying to get a sniff! We are civilised men and we shall not stand for this sort of errant behaviour.'

In this way, Caecilius approached all the men in that place – nearly four hundred in all – and to each one he said, 'We are not flies, buzzing around a pot of old goat meat, trying to get a sniff! We are civilised men and we shall not stand for this sort of errant behaviour.'

This took over two hours and it was only afterwards that Caecilius realised he should have just said, 'We are not flies, buzzing around a pot of old goat meat, trying to get a sniff! We are civilised men and we shall not stand for this sort of errant behaviour' once only, but loud enough so that everybody could hear in one go.

So Caecilius went back to the first man and said

to him, 'I am sorry that took so long. I should have just said, "We are not flies, buzzing around a pot of old goat meat, trying to get a sniff! We are civilised men and we shall not stand for this sort of errant behaviour" once, so that everyone could hear — instead of saying it quietly to each man in turn.'

Then he went up to the second man and said, 'I am sorry that took so long. I should have just said, "We are not flies, buzzing around a pot of old goat meat, trying to get a sniff! We are civilised men and we shall not stand for this sort of errant behaviour" once, so that everyone could hear — instead of saying it quietly to each man in turn.'

And then on to the third man, and so on. This took another three hours, and it was only afterwards that Caecilius realised he should have said, 'I am sorry that took so long. I should have just said, "We are not flies, buzzing around a pot of old goat meat, trying to get a sniff! We are civilised men and we shall not stand for this sort of errant behaviour" once, so that everyone could hear – instead of saying it quietly to each man in turn' once only, instead of saying it to each man in turn.

'OK, I realise I've just wasted about five hours,' said Caecilius. 'Sorry about that.'

'And in that time, more objects have disappeared!' cried Atrium, who had changed his name back to Atrium again. 'See – my marriage ring has been stolen.'

'My golden armband has disappeared!' shouted a thick-set fellow by the name of Wallopus.

'And someone has taken my two-hundred-foot statue of a swan,' exclaimed Filius.

'Then it is just as I thought,' declared Caecilius. 'We have a thief amongst us. Lock the doors, Imperial Shoemakers!'

So the Imperial Shoemakers, so called because they were in charge of locking and unlocking the doors of the public baths, locked the doors. And then Caecilius reared up to his full height and said impressively, 'Look at me, I have reared up to my full height. Now, who is the thief?'

'It is not I,' declared Wallopus.

'Nor I,' asserted Filius.

'And it cannot possibly be I,' said Atrium, 'because – well, it could be I, I suppose. But it is not.'

'And it is not I,' shouted a small man by the name of Smallsupportingcharactus.

'Nor I,' yelled Smallsupportingcharactus's brother, Brotherofsmallsupportingcharactus.

'I am not the thief,' bellowed Bellonicus the grape merchant.

'Nor I!' protested Justmadehimupicus.

'And it was spleffinitely not me, I am blotally

immocint!' protested another man called Mispronunciaticus.

One by one Caecilius's fellow bathers stepped forward to protest their innocence. Until finally, Caecilius's suspicious eye landed on a miserable-looking fellow by the name of Thiefius, who stood cowering in the corner with a Julius Caesar pendant around his neck, a marriage ring on his finger, a golden band around one arm and a two-hundred-foot statue of a swan behind his back.

'Urgh,' said Thiefius, 'Caecilius's suspicious eye just landed on me.' He flicked the eye away and it went bouncing around the walls for a couple of minutes and very nearly got eaten by the vulture, until luckily it pinged back into Caecilius's head just in time, as he had been about to give up hope and replace it with an egg.

'Stop trying to distract us, Thiefius,' said

Caecilius, advancing on the hapless creature. 'It seems that you must be the thief. Because for a start your name is "Thiefius". And also, you seem to have all the objects that have gone missing on or about your person.'

'But I did not do it,' said Thiefius, backing away. 'For though Thiefius is my name, I am an honest man. And also, you know all these objects – the Julius Caesar pendant, the golden armband, the marriage ring and the two-hundred-foot statue of a swan? Well, I came about each of them legitimately and I have a very good explanation for them all.'

'Then let us hear your stories, Thiefius,' said Caecilius, 'for I am not only a fart merchant, I have just remembered that I am the Lord High Judge of Pompeii. If your stories ring true, then you shall be spared prison. But if they sound like lies, then you shall be spared prison.'

'So either way I am spared prison?' said Thiefius.

'Oh, no, sorry,' said Caecilius. 'That was a mistake. If your stories sound like lies then you shall not be spared prison at all. You shall have plenty of prison.'

'OK, that makes a lot more sense,' said Thiefius. And he leant back on the floor, and shot all the bones out of his body so that he was just a big floppy mess of skin and eyes on the floor.

'My first story is how I came by the Julius Caesar pendant,' said Thiefius as his bones danced around the baths, no one really knew why but it was fun to watch. 'And here is my story right now, yes, right now, I'm just carrying on talking because as we've got a little bit more space to fill at the end of this paragraph and I'd quite like my story to begin nicely and neatly on the next page . . . Yes, Caecilius, here comes my first story riiiiiight . . . aboout . . . nearly there . . . NOW.'

THIEFIUS'S
FIRST·STORY:

THIEFIUS·AND·THE
JULIUS·CAESAR·PENDANT

'One day, I think it was a Wednesdonicus or maybe it was a Thursillium, I can't remember,' began Thiefius, 'I decided to visit the Temple of Jupiter. I often go there to steal things, you see, because I am a thief.'

'Aha!' said Caecilius at this, pouncing on Thiefius and stroking his hair, but not fondly. 'You have given yourself away already!'

'No, no, that was just a joke,' said Thiefius, 'of

course I'm not a thief. In fact, I like to visit the Temple of Jupiter to thank him for blessing me with a brilliant sense of humour. If it were not for Jupiter, I would not be able to make jokes about being a thief.'

'I see,' said Caecilius so gravely that a gravestone came out of his eyes. 'Carry on then.'

'Well, up the hill I went to the Temple of Jupiter,' continued Thiefius. 'It was a sunny day and as I went I sang a song about foxes.'

'Let us hear the song,' thundered Caecilius. 'It could be important.'

'OK,' said Thiefius, and he started to sing:

A fox there was, who liked to eat
The grapes upon the vine
He liked to eat
The grapes upon the vine

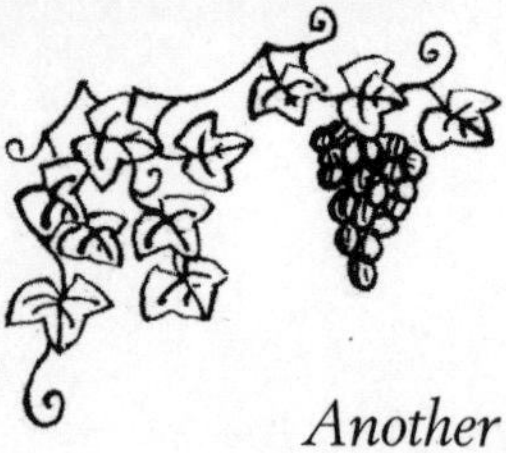

Another fox there was,

who did not like to eat

The grapes upon the vine

He did not like to eat

The grapes upon

the vine

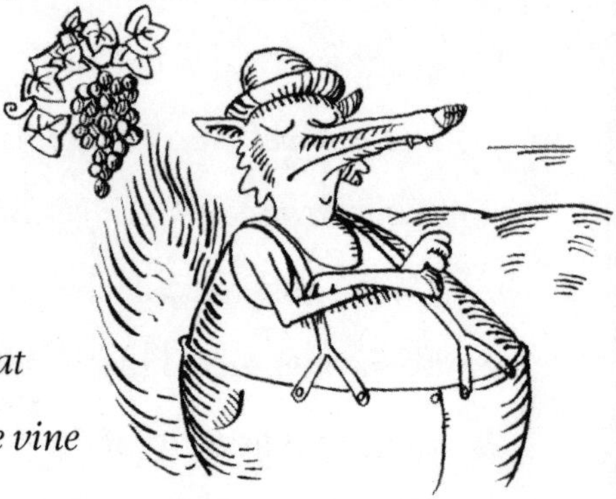

CHORUS:

Some foxes like to eat

The grapes upon the vine

They like to eat

The grapes upon the vine

But

Some other foxes do

not like to eat

The grapes upon the vine

They do not like to eat

The grapes upon the vine

A third fox there was, who liked to eat

The grapes upon the vine

He liked to eat

The grapes upon the vine

In this respect he was quite similar to the first fox

Who liked to eat

The grapes upon the vine

He liked to eat

The grapes upon the vine

CHORUS:

Some foxes like to eat

The grapes upon the vine

They like to eat

The grapes upon the vine

But

Some other foxes do not like to eat

The grapes upon the vine

They do not like to eat

The grapes upon the vine

A fourth fox there was, who did not like to eat

The grapes upon the vine

He did not like to eat

The grapes upon the vine

In this respect he was not very similar to the

first or third foxes but he had more in common

with the second fox

Who did not like to eat

The grapes upon the vine

He did not like to eat

The grapes upon the vine

CHORUS:

Some foxes like to –

'Enough,' commanded Caecilius. 'I was wrong, the song was not important at all. Please continue with your story.'

'Fine,' said Thiefius. 'So anyway, I got to the top of the hill and finally I reached the Temple of Jupiter. Just outside the entrance I found a Julius Caesar pendant lying on the ground. I asked everyone I saw that day if they had dropped a Julius Caesar pendant but they said no. Eventually, unable to find the rightful owner despite my best efforts, I decided that it would not be wrong to claim the pendant for my own. So I swear this pendant around my neck is not yours, Caecilius, for this all happened many years ago, when I was a young man, and I have been wearing it ever since.'

'OK,' said Caecilius. 'You are declared innocent of stealing the Julius Caesar pendant. But how do you account for the marriage ring, Thiefius?'

'Well, there is a simple explanation behind that, my friend,' exclaimed Thiefius. And with that he launched into his second story.

THIEFIUS'S SECOND · STORY:

THIEFIUS · AND · THE MARRIAGE · RING

'This also happened when I was a young man,' began Thiefius, 'and living not in Pompeii but in Rome. Oh, I know that these days I am but a withered old misery with my bones dancing all over the public baths, but back then I was so handsome that I could turn a girl's heart to roses with one look.

Also, I could turn roses into girls' hearts with one look, it was horrible and that is why I was never allowed to enter the Imperial Rose Gardens.

'Anyway, one day I was strolling through Rome turning girls' hearts into roses and singing a song about foxes –'

'Let us hear this song!' commanded Caecilius. 'It could be important.'

'Very well,' said Thiefius, and he began to sing:

A fox there was, who liked to eat
The grapes upon the vine
He liked to eat the grapes –

'Enough,' thundered Caecilius. 'It was not important, it was merely the same song as before. Pray continue.'

'So there I was,' said Thiefius, 'strolling through Rome. I strolled through South Rome, East Rome,

West Rome –'

'What about North Rome?' shrieked Caecilius suspiciously. 'EH?'

'Yes, I was coming to that,' said Thiefius, 'but you interrupted me with your suspicious shriek. I did indeed stroll through North Rome, Caecilius.'

'What about Boofler Rome?' demanded Caecilius. 'Did you stroll through Boofler Rome too?'

'No,' replied Thiefius calmly. 'You see, there is a South Rome, an East Rome, a West Rome and a North Rome. But there is no such place as Boofler Rome, you just made that up in an attempt to catch me out and reveal my story as a lie.'

'I did indeed,' said Caecilius. 'Well done on avoiding my trap, Thiefius, you may have this pelican's skull as a prize.'

'Thank you,' said Thiefius, crunching into the

rare delicacy. 'So there I was, in Rome, remember. And it so happened that a young lady caught my eye. She was beautiful, the most beautiful lady I have ever seen. She had eyes the colour of almonds and lips the colour of strawberries and skin the colour of cream and hair the colour of honey.

'I looked again and realised I had been mistaken. I hadn't been gazing at a woman after all. I had been looking at a big plate of almonds and strawberries topped with cream and honey that a centurion was eating outside a restaurant. But as I continued walking, another young lady caught my eye. And this time it wasn't just a tasty dessert – it was a real woman.'

'What was her name?' screeched Caecilius accusingly.

'It was Melissa,' said Thiefius. 'And once I saw her I asked her to marry me immediately and she

did. And that is why I have this marriage ring upon my withered hand.'

'And where is Melissa now?' rumbled Caecilius.

'Sadly she is dead,' said Thiefius. 'Not a week after we were married, a volcano went off in her stomach and I was left with nothing but Mirror-Men, pencils with rubbers on the end and useless little scraps of her face.'

'Thiefius, I am sorry for your loss,' shouted Caecilius. 'You are found innocent of stealing Atrium's marriage ring. But what of this golden armband? Surely you must have taken it from Wallopus, this very day at the baths?'

'You'd think so, wouldn't you,' said Thiefius. 'But no, for listen to my next story.'

THIEFIUS'S THIRD · STORY:

THIEFIUS · AND · THE GOLDEN · ARMBAND

'When I was a young man I was a restless individual,' began Thiefius, 'and so it was that I joined the crew of a great ship and set to sea. It was a jolly life, Caecilius, full of merriment and carousing.

Many was the night that I and the rest of the crew would sit out on deck beneath the stars, and there we would trade jests and sing songs. In fact, it was while I was aboard this ship that I learnt a fine song, a fine song indeed. And it was a song which I would never forget for the rest of my life.'

'Let us hear it,' roared Caecilius, 'for it could be impor– hold on a moment, was it the one about the foxes?'

'Yes,' said Thiefius.

'OK, never mind about the song,' bellowed Caecilius. 'Please continue.'

'Certainly,' said Thiefius. 'Now, some weeks into our voyage, Neptune himself became angry –'

'Hold on,' said Caecilius, 'do you mean Neptune, the god of the sea, who in his fierce rages can cause the ocean to swell and thrash itself against the rocks, sinking ships and sending thousands of sailors to their deaths? Or do you mean Harry Neptune, who sells peanuts down at the marketplace?'

'I mean Neptune, the god of the sea,' said Thiefius. 'I've never heard of Harry Neptune.'

'OK, sorry,' said Caecilius, 'carry on.'

'But seriously, I can't get my head around what you just said,' said Thiefius. 'I mean really, why would this Harry Neptune guy even *be* in this story? Was he even a sailor before he became a peanut-seller?'

'No, I don't think so,' said Caecilius. 'Look, I said I was sorry, carry on.'

'Very well,' said Thiefius. 'So there we were, some weeks into our voyage, when suddenly Neptune himself – Neptune the god of the sea, *not* Harry Neptune who sells peanuts down at the market,' he added quickly, seeing that Caecilius had lost track again and was about to jump in with a question – 'Neptune became angry and sent down a storm so fierce that it won that year's Fiercest Storm of the Year award. It was terrifying. Terrifying! Terrifying!'

'Was it terrifying?' inquired Caecilius.

'Yes,' said Thiefius. 'Now, during this storm, the ship was tossed and turned on the waves as if it were nothing more than a child's plaything. A hundred sailors died aboard that vessel, which was strange as we'd only started out with seventy-five. In the end, the only survivors were me, Tertius the cook and a slave called Bottaranicusalussalussalussalussalussalu-salussalussalussalussalus. The three of us were washed up on a craggy island and it was there that Bottaranicusalussalussalussalussalussalussalus-salussalussalussalus began his endless questions.

'"What is to become of us?" Bottaranicusalus-salussalussalussalussalusssalussalussalussalus-salus would ask me.

'"I do not know, Bottaranicusalussalussal-ussalussalussalusssalussalussalussalussalussalus," I would reply.

'"But really, what is to become of us?" Bottaran-icusalussalussalussalussalussalusssalussalussalus-salussalussalus would ask me again.

'"I am sorry, Bottaranicusalussalussalussalus-salussalusssalussalussalussalussalussalus, I have just as little idea as you," I would reply. "Now please, Bottaranicusalussalussalussalussalussalusssa-lussalussalussalussalus, stop with all these questions, they are driving me and Tertius mad."

'"OK," said Bottaranicusalussalussalussalus-salussalusssalussalussalussalussalussalus. And then, luckily, he fell into the sea and drowned.

'Now it was just me and Tertius,' continued Thiefius, 'and I must admit, I was scared. There

97

were plenty of herbs and berries on the island, but I could not tell which ones were good to eat and which ones were poisonous.'

'How on earth did you survive?' inquired Caecilius now.

'Well, fortunately, Tertius had been the ship's cook, as I said,' replied Thiefius. 'He knew all

about which herbs and berries were safe to eat, and while he was explaining this, I murdered him and ate him. His body fed me well for days, long enough for another ship to come along and rescue me. And when it did so, the crew gave me a golden armband, which all sailors who have been shipwrecked and yet survived are given as a reward. And that is how I come to have a golden armband.'

'I see,' said Caecilius thoughtfully. 'Well, Thiefius, you have explained yourself very well so far. But there is just one more question I have to put to you – where oh where did you get that two-hundred-foot statue of a swan, that seems incredibly similar to the one my son, Filius, brought to the baths this very day?'

'Ah, that is the easiest of all to explain,' said Thiefius. And he began to tell his final tale.

THIEFIUS'S
FOURTH · STORY:

THIEFIUS · AND · THE
TWO-HUNDRED-FOOT
STATUE · OF · A · SWAN

'To be honest, I did actually steal the two-hundred-foot statue of a swan from Filius,' said Thiefius. 'I'm sorry, I just really wanted it.'

CAECILIUS'S ASTONISHING VERDICT:

'**H**mm,' said Caecilius when the gasps of all the other men in the public baths had finally died down, which didn't take long at all because there were no gasps, they were all asleep, completely bored by the whole affair.

'You have done a brave thing today, Thiefius,' said Caecilius. 'You have owned up to your crime. And seeing that you came by the other items honestly, I have decided to let you off with a warning this time. But be careful that you keep away from crime in the future, Thiefius, because the life of a criminal is unsuitable for a citizen of Pompeii, *capiche?*'

'*Capiche,*' agreed Thiefius.

So Caecilius awoke the Imperial Shoemakers by smashing them in the ribs with a giant golf club, and they unlocked the public baths at last. And everyone ran free and proclaimed, 'Caecilius has judged Thiefius well and truly on this day!'

But Thiefius grinned to himself as he slunk off back to his nest. Because he had actually stolen *all* of those items. And this is why he was called 'Thiefius'. Because he was a thief.

'And I'll be back to hound that poor fool Caecilius again in the future,' he laughed as he went. 'I am the cleverest thief who ever lived.'

THE·END

FILIUS·AND
THE·CURIOUS
OBJECT

Now, one day Filius was playing outside in the street, trying to teach Barkus Wooferinicum to catch frogs, when he happened to spy a curious object lying in the gutter.

I shall not pick it up, he thought.

But then he thought, *No, actually I will.*

But then he thought, *No, I can't really be bothered picking it up. I'll have to walk all the way over to it and it is too hot to do so.*

But then he thought, *But it's only a few steps away.*

But then he thought, *Still, a few steps is a few steps. I honestly can't be bothered.*

But then he thought, *What if I'm missing out? What if I pick it up and it's something really good?*

But then he thought, *But what if it's not something good? I'll have wasted my time and energy.*

But then he thought, *But it might be worth it.*

But then he thought, *But*

it might not be worth it.

But then he thought, *But it's really no big deal, if it's not worth it then who cares, at least I tried.*

But then he thought, *No, I am enjoying my day more than enough already, just me and Barkus Wooferinicum catching frogs on the street. I don't need to know what that curious object is, for the moral of Ancient Pompeii is this:* 'Be content with what you have'.

But then he thought, *But it could lead to an adventure. For the moral of Ancient Pompeii is this:* 'Seize every opportunity for adventure that comes your way'. *That's it, I shall pick it up after all.*

CVI

And so it was that Filius eventually convinced himself to walk over and take a look at the curious object lying in the gutter. But just as he was about to do so, a new thought struck him.

Hang on, he thought. *What if I go over there but when I bend down to see what it is my toga rides up and everyone sees my bottom?*

But then he thought, *What am I worried about? There's no one around to see my bottom.*

But then he thought, *But what if there is someone around after all but they're hiding nearby, hoping that I'll bend over and my toga will ride up and my bottom will pop out and then they laugh at me?*

But then he thought, *It doesn't matter even if there is someone watching, I could go over there and pick up the curious object very carefully, taking great caution all the while to make sure that my bottom stays decent.*

But then he thought, *I'm getting tired of thinking.*

It is growing dark and the Mirror-Men will soon be coming out to hunt. And besides, Barkus Wooferinicum will never learn to catch frogs, in fact some of the frogs have actually caught him.

So Filius spent half an hour or so battling the frogs, who had caught Barkus Wooferinicum in one of their most difficult traps, and eventually he was able to rescue the hound and go inside for supper, which that night was a large cake in the shape of Caecilius. Caecilius got a bit confused by the cake and at one point he started trying to eat himself, but Vesuvius sorted things out by writing 'A CAKE' on the cake using a pencil with a rubber on the end and 'NOT A CAKE' on Caecilius.

A couple of hours later a small girl called Lucia came along and noticed the curious object lying in the gutter. She went over and picked it up and it was the best thing she'd ever found in her life, it was a horse and it became her best friend and it could talk and predict the future and it could fly and it could time travel and it could go to other worlds and it could tell you funny stories and sing songs that were better than any songs ever written and it could play the drums and it could make money and presents come out of its eyes and it could solve all your problems and it could make sure you were never ever lonely ever again and it could make anyone you fancied fall in love with you and it could make you really happy all the time, every second you would be so happy if you picked up that horse, it was unbelievable.

THE·END

THE
CHALLENGE
IN·THE·FORUM

Now, one lunchtime Caecilius was sitting eating a goat in the town square, or the *forum* as the Ancient Romans liked to call it. The day was fine and sunny, because Filius had rolled a I on his dice that morning, and a pleasant breeze rolled in from the coast, tickling Caecilius's toes and making them laugh out loud in his sandals.

It seemed that all Pompeii was going about their business that lunchtime. Bellonicus the grape merchant was doing a roaring trade in grapes. Frinto, who sold lions for the gladiatorial games at the amphitheatre, was doing an even more roaring trade in lions. Two elderly senators called Mayus and Corbynicus stood arguing about politics while Barkus Wooferinicum watched with interest, wondering which of them to bite first. Orticus the swineherd was chasing an escaped piglet round and round in circles; Thiefius was thrusting handfuls of water from the fountain into his pockets when no one was looking; Tambourine the flower-girl was flirting with Onlyappearsinoneotherchapterus the candle-maker; Roscoe Paracetamol, the fiercest soldier in Pompeii, squinted suspiciously at a spiced apple in case it was up to no good; two old men played at cards in the shade of a pillar; a fat baby called Sugarpuffs who no one liked was kicking a milkmaid in the shin . . .

The air fizzled and popped with the sounds, sights and smells of the city, and as Caecilius sat there munching his goat in the sunshine, he felt he had never been so glad to be alive. (Except he wished his toes would stop giggling, they were getting on his nerves a bit.)

Presently, Caecilius's ugly friend Atrium strolled over and sat himself down beside the fart merchant. '*Salve*, Caecilius,' said Atrium, helping himself to rather a large bite of goat. 'Buzzle-swuzzle for your thoughts?'

'Oh, *salve*, Atrium,' smiled Caecilius. 'I was just having one of those moments where everything seems just right. Do you know what I mean? When the whole world seems completely in tune with itself.'

'Oh yes?' said Atrium, who knew that when Caecilius was in a philosophical mood like this you could get loads of goat off him without him even noticing.

'I mean,' laughed Caecilius, 'you spend your whole life trying to make an honest buzzle, worrying about success, worrying about taxes, worrying about the government . . .'

'Um hum,' nodded Atrium, biting into a mouthful of shin.

'But what really counts is the simple stuff, Atrium. Family. Companionship. The smell of freshly baked bread in the marketplace . . . Just sitting here watching the world go about its business, I am filled with such a sense of peace, Atrium! Such a sense of contentment! Such a love for all human life! Yes, I think that's it, really, that's what it comes down to – a love for all human life.'

'Beautifully put,' burped Atrium, finishing off the last of the goat and wiping his gob on Caecilius's toga. 'You should be a poet. Hey, by the way, have you seen that stupid face someone's drawn on the moon? "Bibbling Ted" or something? By Jupiter, it's useless! It looks more like a pile of cat sick than a face. I wonder who did it.'

'How dare you!' yelled Caecilius, starting to his feet in anger. 'My own wife drew that face! You have gone too far this time, Atrium! You have insulted Vesuvius's honour and I challenge you to a duel to the death!'

'Hey!' said Atrium. 'What about all that "love of human life" stuff?'

'Shut up, you detestable flea!' spat Caecilius.

'Do you accept my challenge, Atrium? Or are you the coward I always took you for?'

'I am no coward!' bleated Atrium, who had been busy running away as fast as he could and had made it halfway up an olive tree. 'Very well, I accept your stupid challenge, you absolute lump!'

'Then we shall meet back here at dawn, when the cockerel crows,' said Caecilius. 'You had better get a good night's sleep, Atrium – for it shall be your last.'

'How was the forum today?' asked Vesuvius when Caecilius arrived home some hours later. 'Anything interesting happen?'

'No, not really,' shrugged Caecilius. 'Just the usual – Oh no, hang on, I challenged Atrium to a duel to the death.'

'What!' cried Vesuvius. 'What on earth were you thinking?'

'Well, he was insulting you,' said Caecilius, 'and I couldn't bear it and, I don't know, it just popped out.'

'How exactly did he insult me?' said Vesuvius.

'He was making fun of that face you drew on the

moon,' said Caecilius. 'He said it looked like a pile of cat sick.'

'Fair enough,' said Vesuvius. 'He's entitled to his opinion.'

'How dare you, Vesuvius!' shouted Caecilius. 'You have the nerve to say that Atrium is entitled to his opinion? You have insulted Vesuvius's honour, Vesuvius, and I challenge you to a duel to the death!'

'Caecilius,' sighed Vesuvius. 'Please stop challenging everyone to a duel to the death.'

'Well, you see how easily it can happen,' said Caecilius. 'It just pops out.'

'That may be so,' said Vesuvius, 'but let me go and talk to Atrium. I am sure that he will listen to reason and we can fix things without anyone getting hurt.'

'OK,' said Caecilius. 'What shall I do while you are gone?'

'Why don't you dress up as a weasel?' suggested Vesuvius, who knew that Caecilius sometimes enjoyed dressing up as a weasel.

So Caecilius dressed up as a weasel and sat there in the front room waiting for Vesuvius to return. *What a big silly I've been!* he thought as he played with his whiskers. *How fortunate I am to have such a level-headed wife as Vesuvius!*

Presently the front door flew open with a loud bang and in stormed Vesuvius, muttering and cursing under her breath.

'How did it go, darling?' said Caecilius, fluffing his tail alluringly.

'Not brilliantly,' scowled Vesuvius. 'You see, while I was trying to convince Atrium to see sense, Hortus started sticking her nose in, boasting about her scented herb gardens and whatnot, and I ended up challenging her to a duel to the death.'

CXVIII

'Oh, Vesuvius,' sighed Caecilius. 'Dear, good-natured Vesuvius. 'This is nothing but a simple misunderstanding between women. Wait here, I will go and talk to Hortus. I shall soon have this all cleared up.'

※　⁂　※

'How did it go, husband?' said Vesuvius when Caecilius returned some time later.

'Not very well,' admitted Caecilius, a little sheepishly; but quite a lot more weaselishly, because he had forgotten to take off his weasel costume. 'While I was trying to calm Hortus down, Atrium got angry and challenged you to a duel to the death. Then I got angry at Hortus and challenged *her* to a duel. Also to the death. Actually, from now on let's stop saying "duel to the death" and just say "duel" for short, because it's going to be coming up quite a lot in conversation in the next few minutes, OK?'

'Let me get this straight,' said Vesuvius. 'You've challenged Atrium to a duel. I've challenged Hortus to a duel. Atrium has challenged me to a duel. And you've challenged Hortus to a duel.'

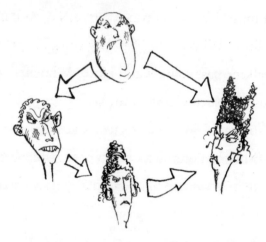

'Exactly,' said Caecilius. 'But that's not all. You see, while I was challenging Hortus to a duel, that blasted fool Neptune walked past – '

'Hold on,' said Vesuvius, 'do you mean Harry Neptune, who sells peanuts down at the marketplace?

Or do you mean Neptune, the god of the sea, who in his fierce rages can cause the ocean to swell and thrash itself against the rocks, sinking ships and sending thousands of sailors to their deaths?'

'I mean Harry Neptune who sells peanuts,' said Caecilius. 'Why would Neptune, the god of the sea, be walking past Atrium and Hortus's house?'

'I suppose not,' said Vesuvius.

'Anyway, Harry Neptune walked past and he joined in the argument and ended up challenging Atrium, Hortus and you to a duel.'

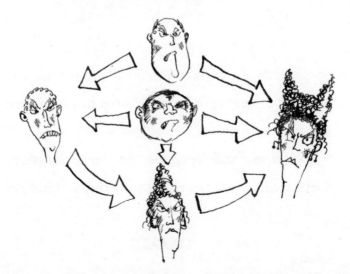

'Why didn't he challenge you to a duel too?' said Vesuvius indignantly.

'I don't know,' said Caecilius. 'He just didn't. Anyway, so then Filius walked past and challenged Harry Neptune to a duel.'

'No!' cried Vesuvius.

'Yes,' said Caecilius. 'But it gets worse, for at that moment I took leave of my senses and challenged Filius to a duel.'

'Our own son!' gasped Vesuvius. 'Why, Caecilius, why?'

'I am sorry,' said Caecilius. 'But I felt obliged to defend Harry Neptune's honour, seeing as Harry Neptune hadn't challenged *me* to a duel. I felt I owed him that, at least. So yes, I challenged Filius to a duel. It just popped out, I'm afraid.'

'And after that,' continued Caecilius sadly, 'well, Vesuvius, all hell broke loose. Hortus challenged Barkus Wooferinicum to a duel. Barkus Wooferinicum challenged some frogs to a duel. A couple of chickens challenged you to a duel, Vesuvius, I think you should be able to win that one though, they should be quite easy to beat, you should just be able to step on them, with a bit of luck. And then – you know that little baby? Sugarpuffs?'

'Oh yes,' said Vesuvius. 'I hate him.'

'Everybody does,' said Caecilius. 'Anyway, Sugarpuffs stuck his head out of a window and started getting involved and then Bellonicus stuck *his* head out of a window and challenged the whole street to a duel and then some more people from the next street stuck *their* heads out of their windows and, well, you see, Vesuvius, the thing is . . . In one way or another everyone in Pompeii has now challenged everyone else to a duel to the death.'

'Oh, Caecilius,' wept Vesuvius, throwing herself down on the couch. 'Do you see how quickly your anger has spread?'

'Yes,' said Caecilius. 'Quite quickly.'

'Our entire town is at war with one another,' lamented Vesuvius. 'And all because of Bobbling Ed.'

'Maybe we should run away until this has all blown over,' suggested Caecilius.

'Certainly not,' said Vesuvius. 'Running away is never the answer.'

'What about if you're being chased by a monster?' said Caecilius, who had once been chased by a monster, except no one ever believed him.

'Not that again,' said Vesuvius. 'No, husband, there is nothing for it, for the moral of Ancient Pompeii is this: "*Finish what you start*". We must honour the challenges that have been thrown down. We must face what we have done.'

'Then Jupiter help us,' said Caecilius, his whiskers drooping miserably. 'Jupiter help us all.'

※ ※ ※

Spears. Swords. Boulders. Barrels. Sticks. Stones. Bricks. Bones. Boots. Vases. Plant pots. Arrows. Trained wasps. Daggers. The vulture. Carpet beaters. Other things. The people of Pompeii had brought to the battle anything and everything they could lay their hands on. Roscoe Paracetamol's sword hung ominously from his belt. Sugarpuffs had a rattle with spikes all over it and a sling made from a dirty nappy, ready to fire rocks and poos at his enemies. He really was the most atrocious baby you could imagine.

From the stone steps at the north end of the forum, Caecilius gazed out at the vast crowd below.

'They're getting restless,' whispered Vesuvius. 'Come on, Caecilius. You can do this.'

'Why don't *you* address the crowd instead, Vesuvius?' he gulped. 'I'm not scared or anything, it's just . . . My throat's gone a bit dry, that's all.'

'I believe in you, Father,' said Filius. 'For you are my inspiration and my light.'

'Thank you for having faith in me, son,' said Caecilius, stroking Filius's hair fondly. 'I'm sorry that in a few minutes' time we'll have to fight each other to the death. What weapons did you bring to try and kill me with, by the way?'

'A large sword, Father,' said Filius. 'And a plank with a nail through it. And a whip.'

'Drat and figs,' muttered Caecilius. 'You're probably going to win then, I only brought a tennis ball.'

'A tennis ball?' said Filius. 'You'll never kill me with that, what were you thinking?'

'I got confused,' whispered Caecilius.

'Come, husband, your public awaits,' said Vesuvius. 'You can worry about slaughtering your only child later.'

A hush descended as Caecilius turned towards the crowd and threw his arms out wide.

'Citizens of Pompeii!' he cried. 'Hear my words and hear them well! Know that on this day, I, Caecilius Maximus Panini the fart merchant, have come to this place to do battle with Atrium Jamiroquai Tannicus the ship-owner! We are here to enter into a duel to the death, I can't remember who started it but I think it was probably Atrium.'

'Hey!' shouted Atrium but everyone ignored him.

'And know too,' continued Caecilius, 'that Atrium's cowardly challenge –'

'Hey!' shouted Atrium again.

'Atrium's cowardly challenge has led to many more challenges!' roared Caecilius. 'I tried to stop him, for I am a man of peace! But he would not listen to reason and that is why we are all gathered here today, I'm sorry but that's how it is, it's all Atrium's fault that we're going to die and I vote that he should forever be remembered as "The Greatest Traitor in All of History".'

'Hey!' shouted Atrium again.

'In all probability, none of us shall leave this place alive,' said Caecilius. 'If anyone would like to say any final words, please step up here right now and let us hear them, no, not you, Atrium, you have already caused far too much trouble and we are no longer interested in your vile excuses. No one? Very well then, let us proceed.

'Look at this cage I have strapped to my head,' cried Caecilius, 'for it contains the town cockerel, Lester. I was going to suggest that we wait until Lester crows to announce dawn – and that then the duelling should begin. But unfortunately Lester is dead. You see, I challenged him to a duel on the way here and – well, like I said, he's dead now. Sorry, everyone.'

'Why are you even wearing that cage then?'
shouted someone. 'What's the point?'

'What's the point of anything, when you really
think about it?' explained Caecilius. 'Now,' he said,
tossing Lester the cockerel's mangled body into a
ditch, where it immediately burrowed deep into

the nourishing soil and was reincarnated as a family of moles. 'Everyone – take your marks! I shall count to XX and with each number you are all to take another step from your opponent. At the XXth step I shall cry "TURN AND FIRE!" And then . . . Well, then, my friends, our fates are in the laps of the Gods. Good luck, everyone. Except all the people who are trying to kill me, obviously.'

Overhead, the sky was sullen and grey. The great buildings seemed to frown down in solemn judgement as Caecilius began his count. In the distance the volcano coughed once and was silent.

'I,' counted Caecilius.

Everyone turned and took a pace away from their opponent.

'II,' counted Caecilius.

Another pace.

'III,' counted Caecilius.

'VI,' counted Caecilius, 'sorry, I mean IV, I always get those II mixed up.

'V,' counted Caecilius.

'VI,' counted –

But at that moment a small boy rushed forward from the crowd, bounded up the great stone steps III at a time, and shoved the fart merchant roughly aside.

'Stop this madness!' he cried. 'Stop this madness, I beg you!'

A great roar of confusion swept through the crowd. Who could possibly be so important that they had the nerve to interrupt the proceedings? A visiting king? The Emperor? Perhaps Mars, the god of War and Snacking Between Mealtimes, had seen fit to come down to earth and take matters into his own chocolatey hands. But no. It was none of those dudes.

'Slavius!' gasped Caecilius in astonishment.

'How dare you, what on earth do you think you are up to! I challenge you to a du–'

But Slavius shook his head.

'No, master,' said Slavius. 'As well you know, the law forbids any slave from entering into a duel to the death. For, unlike you, we slaves are not free to play with our own lives. As slaves, our lives do not belong to us – but to the Holy Roman Empire itself.'

'You seem to know a lot about law and things all of a sudden,' grumbled Caecilius, but Slavius went on.

'Citizens of Pompeii!' he cried. 'As a slave, my life is worth next to nothing! I am an outsider from society! But, oh, we outsiders see much with our poor eyes that you may miss with your more expensive ones!

'We slaves serve you at every moment from dawn to dusk, Pompeii! We keep your togas ironed and your sandals polished! We keep your water fresh and your food hot and your floors sparkling and your streets swept and your hair brushed and your fingernails cut and your noses clean of the Mirror-Men who occasionally crawl up in there while you are asleep, I bet you didn't know that, did you? But we do. We are always cleaning Mirror-Men out of your noses. Just the other day I found about forty of them in Filius's left nostril, it was revolting.

'Anyway, where was I? Oh, yes. As we go about our work, Pompeii, we see every inch of this great and majestic city, and all that happens within its walls! From the extravagant dinner parties on which we are forced to attend, serving up your farts and sweetmeats without complaint; to the lowly Tavern of the Slaves, which you fine ladies and gentlemen would shudder to enter! From the shining dome of the Temple of Jupiter high upon the hill; to the filthiest hovel in the slums, where hens and vagabonds lie vomiting in the gutter! From the red wine that flows so freely in your villas; to the slushy grey sewage that runs in your drains! We slaves see it all!

'You push us around like beans on a plate but we slaves are the very lifeblood that keeps your city functioning! We are the heart that keeps Pompeii marching forward! We are the memory of Pompeii! We are the conscience of Pompeii! Citizens, we slaves *are* Pompeii!

'So,' finished Slavius, gazing down at every face in the crowd, and seeming to see into each and every soul. 'If you truly are determined to go through with this madness, then at least have the courage to admit that you are taking not only your own lives – but the life of the city itself! Kill *me*, citizens!'

'What!' cried the crowd, who had listened to Slavius's speech as if spellbound. 'Kill you! A mere boy? Unarmed and defenceless? It is not right!'

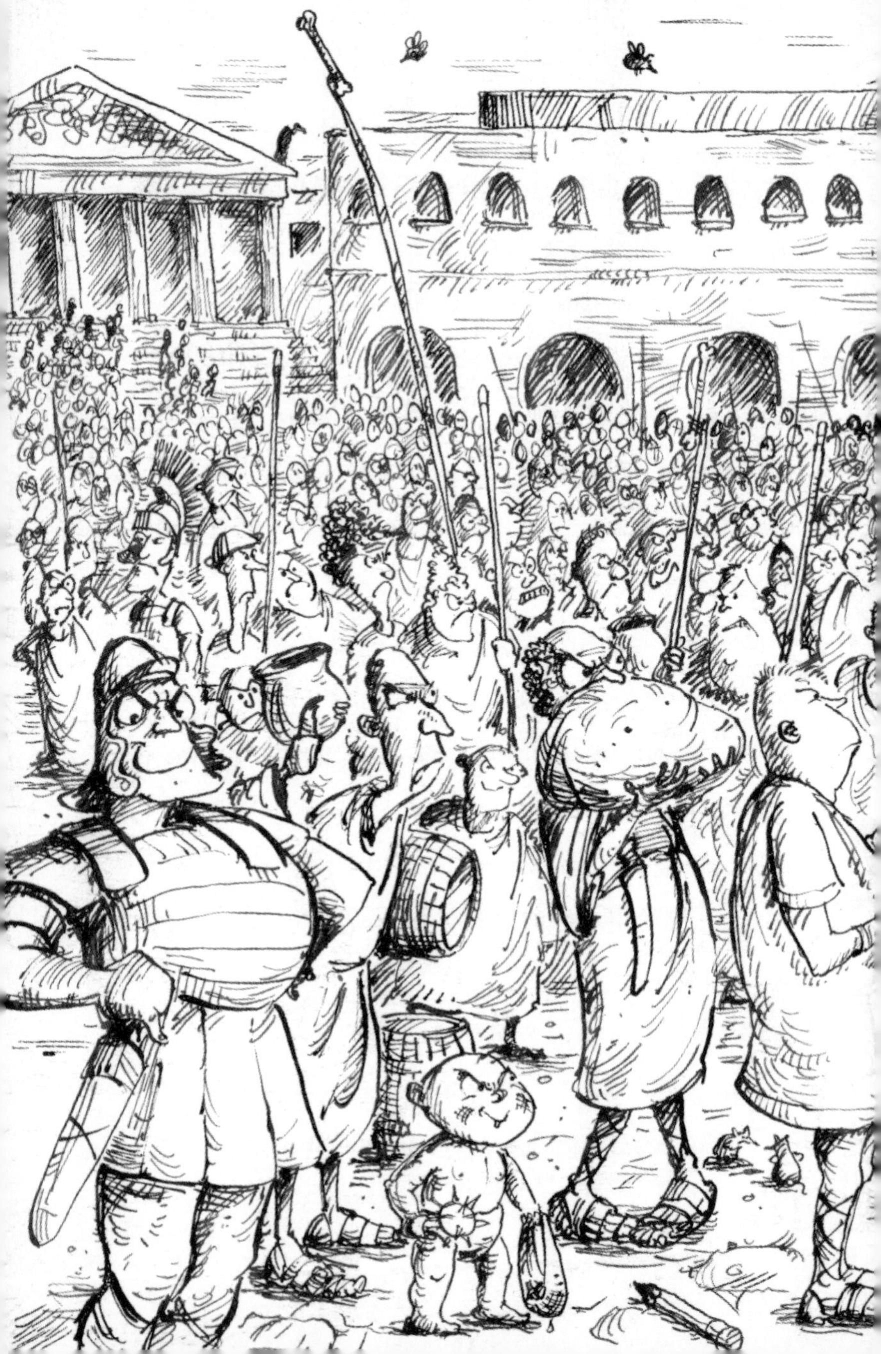

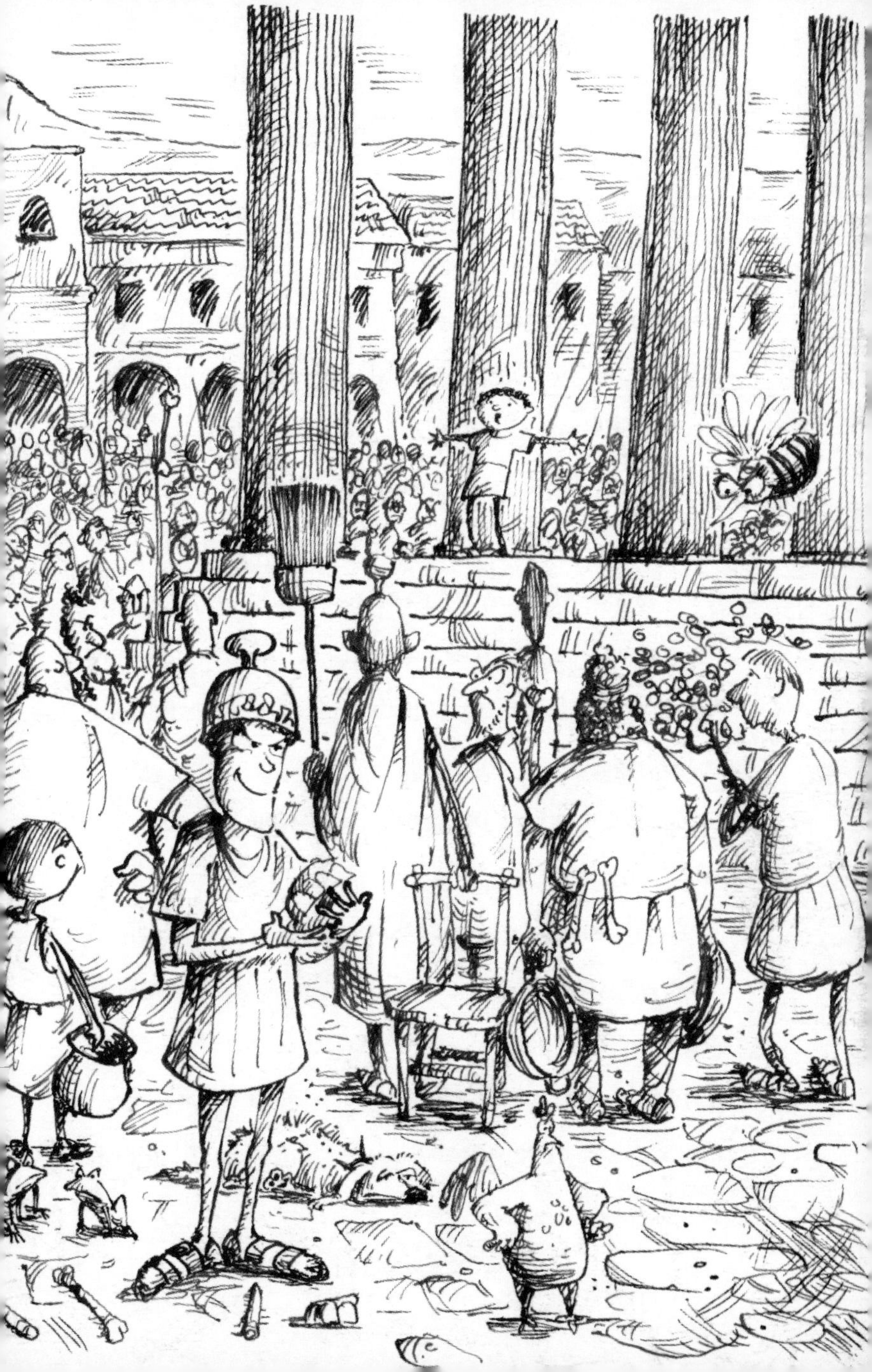

'You heard me,' said Slavius. 'Kill me. For in killing me, you shall be killing all of Pompeii. See! I fall to my knees to make it all the easier for you. Kill me, kill me now! End my life! Strike me down on this spot like a rabid dog.

'Kill me! Kill me, I dare you! Come on, Atrium, use that big stick you came here with today! Poke me in the face with it until I'm all red and squooshy! Kill me, Filius! Take your dagger and strike me through the heart! Kill me, Caecilius, take that tennis ball and – hang on, seriously?'

'Look, I got confused, all right?' said Caecilius in embarrassment.

'Well, ask that guy for his spear then,' said Slavius. 'That guy over there, Caecilius, that one over there with the funny ears. Go on! Ask that guy if you can borrow his spear and then shove it right through my brains, I don't even care! Squish that spear all about in my brains in front of everybody if life truly means so little to you.

'No? Then how about you, Vesuvius? Kill me like you are squashing an ant beneath your sandal! You can even get a giant sandal if you want and stand on me and call me an ant while you do it, I don't care! Or you, Orticus. Kill me up, slice me from top to bottom like one of your pigs for market!

'Perhaps you, Bellonicus? Pop my head like a grape, why don't you? Roscoe Paracetamol! Want to have a go? You're supposed to be such a mighty soldier, come on then, show us how it's done! Or you, Harry Neptune. Crack my head open as if you are shelling a peanut, mmm, tasty!

'Kill me, everyone! Kill me, Pompeii! Kill me a thousand times over, kill me ten thousand times over! Splam me up! Do me in! End my days! Shove me off! Stop my clock! Run me through! KILL ME,

POMPEII! FOR I AM EVERYTHING THAT YOU SEEK TO DESTROY TODAY!'

And then Slavius said no more, but simply put his face in his hands and wept, not for himself, but for the madness of the crowd and things.

'All right, all right,' said Caecilius, who like everyone else had listened to this extraordinary speech in some amazement. 'Calm down, Slavius, what on earth's got into you. We won't do any of those duels then, if you feel so strongly about it.'

'Thanks,' said Slavius. 'Hey, can we get some food, I'm starving?'

'Not right now,' said Caecilius. 'I'll get you a sandwich or something back at the villa.'

'What, not eat?' cried Slavius, falling at his master's feet and tearing his toga open to expose his bare chest. 'Then kill me! Kill me now, Caecilius, for though I am merely a slave, I would rather die than go hungry a second longer! Here, grab that rock over there and pound the very life from my skull! Kill me now, Caecilius, kill me where I kneel! Ki – '

'Slavius,' frowned Caecilius. 'Don't push it.'

'Citizens of Pompeii,' said Caecilius. 'It has taken the lowest and smelliest amongst us to divert us from this course of destruction and we should be humbled.'

'We are,' moaned the crowd. 'Oh, how we are humbled.'

'We have learned our lesson,' said Caecilius, helping Slavius to his feet. 'We are truly grateful, each and every –'

A poo went whizzing past Caecilius's ear.

'Well, nearly each and every one of us is grateful,' said Caecilius. 'Sugarpuffs, stop that at once, no one is impressed. Now, what shall we do to make sure this never happens again?'

'Let us make duels to the death illegal from this moment on!' shouted Hortus. 'Take it to the vote!'

'An excellent notion,' said Caecilius. 'All of those in favour – say "aye"! Now all of those against, say "nay"! The vote is passed! For despite Atrium's insatiable lust for violence and revenge –'

'Hey!' shouted Atrium.

'Despite that, wiser heads have prevailed.'

'And we should make Slavius a free boy!' shouted Harry Neptune. 'For he alone has saved all of us, he save every one of us, he save every one of us, every man, every woman, every peanut, Flash!'

'Yes, release the lad from his servitude!' agreed Bellonicus. 'Take it to the vote, Caecilius!'

'An excellent notion,' said Caecilius. 'All in favour of making Slavius a free boy, say "aye"! Now, all those who are against the idea – say "nay"! OK, let me just do a few quick sums on my fingers . . . Well, Slavius, it was extremely close, but in the end the idea was voted down. You're still a slave, I'm afraid.'

'Bad luck, Slavius,' said Filius. 'Here, lick my sandal clean, there's a tiny spot of dirt on it.'

And so Caecilius and Vesuvius and Filius and Barkus Wooferincum stood proudly upon the forum steps while Slavius knelt in the dust, licking Filius's sandal clean, and all was well in the city of Pompeii. Caecilius declared a national holiday and somehow everyone in all the other towns and countries heard him declare it, so the whole of the Holy Roman Empire did nothing that afternoon but laze around in the sun swallowing farts and drinking wine, not the children, they weren't allowed wine, of course, except Sugarpuffs managed to climb into a barrel of the stuff and spent the rest of the day completely drunk and trying to fight a building.

And as afternoon turned to evening and evening to night, there was great rejoicing in the forum amongst Paninis and non-Paninis alike.

And the moon rose, big and bright and full, and they all felt very small beneath it. And Bobbling Ed gazed down upon the people of Pompeii, and there they all sat, looking up at him and thinking about all the trouble he had caused them and all the lessons they had ended up learning.

'Ah, 'Suvie,' sighed Caecilius, stroking his wife's hair fondly. 'What a day it's been. But despite all the heartache and worry, I think we have emerged as better, wiser people, especially me, you did OK, Vesuvius – but I *really* improved my

character and I am now one of the wisest and most spectacular men on earth. For the moral of Ancient Pompeii is this,' he continued, drawing Vesuvius's face to his and planting a tender kiss on his wife's lips. '"*Let us mend our differences not with swords – but with love*".'

THE·EN-

'Hang on a minute,' said Atrium. 'I've just thought of something.'

'Can't you see we're having a romantic moment, Atrium?' said Vesuvius. 'Give a married couple some peace, why don't you?'

'Yes, but –' said Atrium. 'Look, it's a full moon tonight, right?'

'What of it?' said Caecilius.

'Well, how come you didn't turn into the ma-wol-n-f again, Caecilius?' said Atrium.

'I don't know,' shrugged Caecilius. 'I just didn't. I don't turn into the ma-wol-n-f every time there's a full moon, you know.'

'But does it have to be a full moon for it to happen in the first place?' said Atrium.

'Yes,' said Caecilius.

'But it doesn't happen every full moon?'

'No,' said Caecilius. 'Sometimes it does and

sometimes it doesn't. There's not really any rule to it as far as I can see.'

'Why not?' frowned Atrium. 'It doesn't make sense.'

'Drat and figs, man!' said Caecilius. 'Leave us alone. For the moral of Ancient Pompeii is this: *"Shut up, Atrium, no one cares what you think".'*

THE·END

LEARN·LATIN·
WITH·CAECILIUS

*S*alve, everyoneicus! Did you enjoy those stories about me and my family and my friends and that idiot, Atrium? Of course you did, you're only human. But the astonishing truth is that all those stories actually happened not in 'English', whatever that is – but in 'Latin', which is what we speak here in Ancient Pompeii. And now it is time to learn Latin with me, because not only am I a fart merchant, I am a powerful teacher of languages and I have got one of those little hats with a dangly bit which tickles your nose to prove it.

First you will need to learn some basic words and phrases. So – let's get started!

Hello
Salve

Goodbye
Vale

Hello again
Salve iterum

Goodbye again
Iterum vale

Hey, how come when I typed 'hello again' into Google Translate it put the 'salve' bit first and the 'iterum' bit second, but when I typed 'goodbye again' it put the 'iterum' bit first and the 'salve' bit second? *Heus tu, quam cum typus 'salve iterum' in Google Translate et pone 'salve' mortes primo et 'iterum' aliquantulus secundus, sed quando ego typed in 'vale iterum' et pone 'iterum' aliquantulus prima et 'salve' secundam partem?*

Languages are weird
Linguae sunt cerritulus

Oh no, I've hit the wrong button, I think it's doing German now
Oh nein, ich habe den falschen Knopf gedrückt, ich denke es macht jetzt Deutsch

Drat and figs! Now it's doing Portuguese
Drat e figos! Agora está fazendo Português

Hang on a minute, let me fix this
Espere um minuto, deixe-me corrigir isso

Oops
唉呀

How do you work this thing?
這到底要怎麼弄啊?

Vesuvius, can you give me a hand?
It's all going a bit wrong
維蘇威, 你可以幫我一下嗎?
總是弄不對

Vesuvius?
維蘇威？

Vesuvius?
維蘇威？

Vesuvius!
維蘇威！

Where is that woman?
這女人去哪兒了？

I'm glad we don't really have computers in Ancient
Pompeii, they're a complete waste of time
我真慶幸我們古代龐貝城的時候沒有電腦，
它完全是在浪費時間

Chinese words look a bit like 'Shreddies',
don't they?
中文字真有點像 " Shreddies "，是吧？

VESUVIUS!
維蘇威！

Forget it, I'm going to bed
算了, 我還是去睡覺吧

Have you read all the

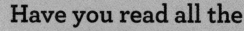

MR GUM

books?

They're WELL BRILLIANT!

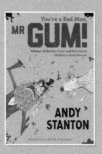

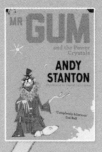

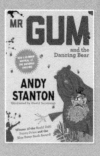

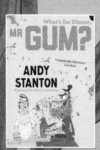

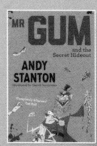

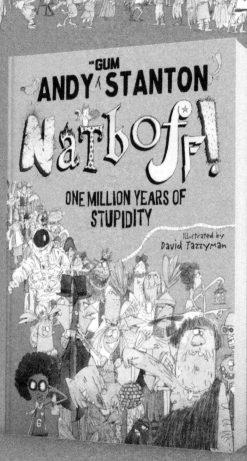

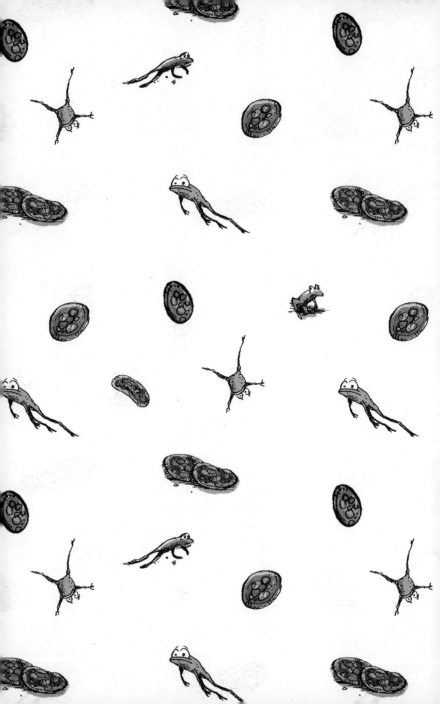

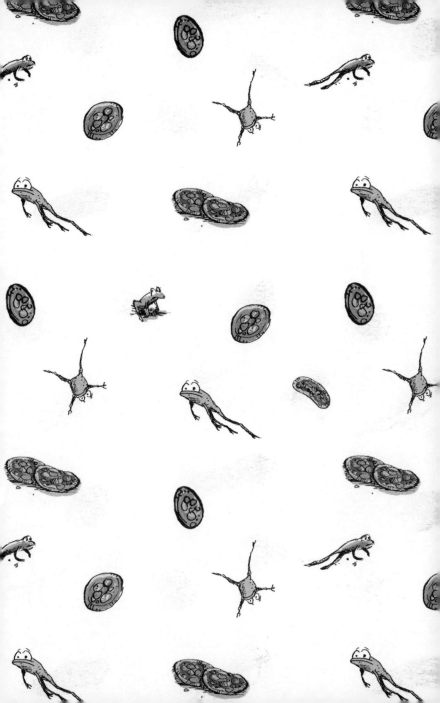

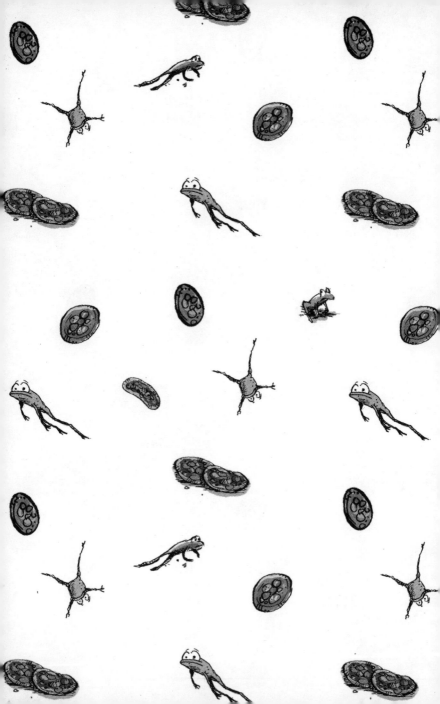